The Bike Lesson

Come here, Small Bear.
Here is something
you will like.

Look, Ma, look!
A brand-new bike.

Thanks, Dad! Thanks!
For me, you say?
I am going to ride it
right away!

Not yet, not yet,
not yet, my son . . .

First come the lessons,
then the fun.
How to get on is
lesson one.

Lesson one?

Is that lesson one?

Yes.
That is what
you should not do.
So let that be a
lesson to you.

Yes it was, Dad.
Now I see.
That was a very good
lesson for me.

Dad! Where are you going?
You showed me how.
Why don't you let me
ride it now?

Not yet. Not yet.
Before you do
I'll have to give you
lesson two.

Just watch, Small Bear.
Just watch your Pop.
Lesson two is
how to stop.

A very good lesson.
Thank you, Pop.

May I ride it now
that you showed me how?
May I?
May I ride it now?

Not yet. Not yet.
You have more to learn.
I'll have to show you
how to turn.

Just watch me . . .

DANGER

This is lesson
number three.

Wow! What a lesson!
That number three!
That may be a little
too hard for me.

This is what
you must never do.
Now let this be
a lesson to you.

It surely was, Dad!
Now I see.
That was a very good
lesson for me.

When I get you down
may I ride it then?
May I? May I?
Just say when.

Wait, my son.
You must learn some more.
I have yet to teach
you lesson four.

When you come to a puddle
what will you do?
Will you go around
or ride right through?

It's not so good
to ride right through.

You're right, Dad.
I can clearly see
why that lesson
was good for me.

When I get you out,
may I ride it then?
Please, Dad . . .
Will you tell me when?

Of course. You may ride it.
You can. You will.

. . . After lesson five.

How to go down hill.

Wow! What a lesson!
That looks hard,
going down hill
through a chicken yard.

Dad, please tell me . . . will I
ever ride it?
Or will I just keep
running beside it?

Will I?
Will I?
Will I?
When?

Pretty soon, Son.
But not just yet.
There is still one lesson
you have to get.
Lesson six is
the hardest yet.

To be a good rider,
to really know how,
you will have to learn
about safety now.

To be safe, Small Bear,
when you ride a bike,
you can not just take
any road you like.

Before you take one
you must know . . .

. . . where that road
is going to go.

See?
This is what
you should not do.
Now let this be
a lesson to you.

It surely was, Dad.
Now I see.
That was another good
lesson for me.

May I ride it now?
May I ride it now?

After one more lesson.
It will be the last.
There is one more thing.
I can teach it fast.

When I ride on a road
I take great pride
in always riding
on the left hand side.

But, Dad!
Are you riding
on the left hand side?

I guess I know
my hands, Small Bear.
My right is here.
My left is there.

Or am I wrong?

Now could that be?

Left hand . . . ? Right hand . . . ?

Let me see . . .

Left hand on the
left hand side . . .
Right hand on the
right hand side.

Thank you, Pop!
You showed me how.
But, please
please
PLEASE
may I ride it now?

Look, Ma!

Now I can ride it!

See!

Dad had some very good lessons for me.